SiMPLY
RiDiCULOUS

RETOLD BY
virginia davis

ILLUSTRATED BY
russ willms

KIDS CAN PRESS LTD.
TORONTO

Kids Can Press Ltd. acknowledges with appreciation the
assistance of the Canada Council and the Ontario Arts Council
in the production of this book.

Canadian Cataloguing in Publication Data
Davis, Virginia, 1933-
Simply ridiculous
ISBN 1-55074-107-1
I. Willms, Russ. II. Title.
PS8557.A85S5 1995   jC 813'.54   C95-930523-8
PZ7.D38Si 1995

Kids Can Press Ltd.
29 Birch Avenue
Toronto, Ontario, Canada
M4V 1E2

Edited by Debbie Rogosin
Designed by Russ Willms
Typeset by Nancy Yeasting – Suburbia Studios
Printed and bound in Hong Kong by
Wing King Tong Company Limited

95 0 9 8 7 6 5 4 3 2 1

To my father, because he loved language and read to us
every night at the dinner table

To Ryan and Taylor

R W

In a village far, far away, there lived a young man who was sometimes a little silly. One day his wife came to him and said, "Willy, we're going to have a child."

"Oh, wife," Willy cried happily, "what kind of child will we have?"

"Well, husband, I don't know," she replied.

"You don't know?" grumbled Willy. He thought for a time and said, "But I want to know now. I will go to see the Wise Old Man. He will tell me."

So Willy took a cow as a gift and went up the hills to the mountain of the Wise Old Man.

The old man saw him coming and called out, "Have you come to partake of my wisdom?"

"Yes," said Willy. "I need your help."

"Well, come in, sit down, and tell me your troubles."

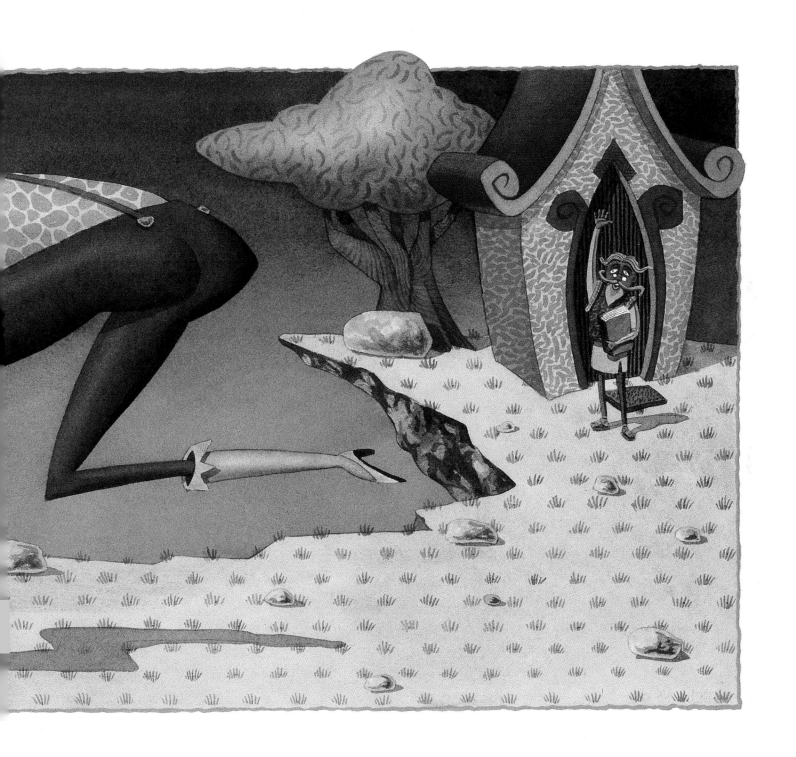

So Willy did. He told how he had grown to be a young man and had fallen in love and married. Now he was to be a father. But his wife could not tell him what kind of child they would have, and he had come to the Wise Old Man to find out.

The old man smiled. "I think I can help," he said. He took a jar of beans and sprinkled them on the ground. Then, for a long time, he stared deeply into the beans.

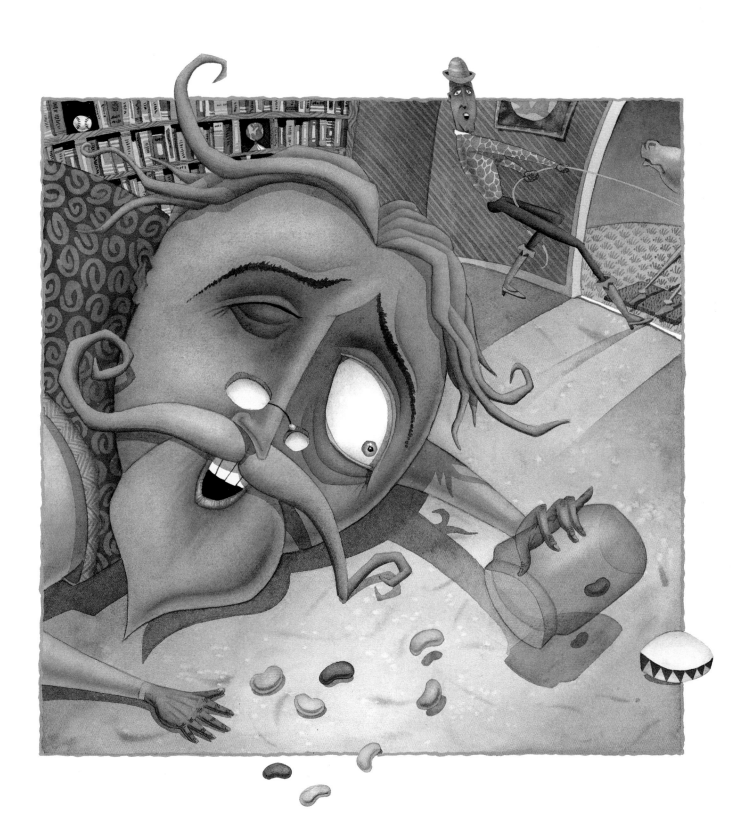

"Hmmmmmmmmmm," he said quietly.
"Hmmmmmmmmmm," echoed Willy.
"Ohhhhhhhhhhhhh," he said sagely.
"Ohhhhhhhhhhhhh," echoed Willy.
"AhhhHHHHHHHHHHH," he said loudly.
"AhhhHHHHHHHHHHH," echoed Willy.

Finally the old man said, "Come closer,
and I will tell you what kind of child you
will have."

Willy moved closer.

The old man looked at him kindly
and declared, "You will have either a girl
or a boy."

Willy was elated, and he rushed home to tell his wife.

After a time the child was born, and it was indeed ... a boy.

Willy and his wife were overjoyed. "How wise the old man was," said Willy. "Now we must give our son a very special name."

But each time Willy thought of a name, it wasn't quite right. And each time his wife suggested a name, it wasn't quite right either.

"I know what I must do," said Willy one day. "I must go again to see the Wise Old Man. He will tell us the name of our child."

So once more Willy took a cow and went up the hills to the mountain of the Wise Old Man.

"Ah," the old man greeted him. "Have
you come to partake further of my wisdom?"
"Yes," said Willy. "I need your help now
more than ever."
"Well, come in, sit down, and tell me
your troubles."
"My wife," said Willy, "had our child.
And it was, just as you told us, a boy.
We decided that for our son there must be a
very special name. But we have thought
and thought and cannot find the name.
So I have come to you, hoping
you will know the name
of our child."

The old man nodded and
said, "Yes, I think I can help you."
Again he took a jar of beans,
sprinkled them on the ground,
and stared deeply into them.

"Hmmmmmmmmm," he said quietly.
"Hmmmmmmmmm," echoed Willy.
"Ohhhhhhhhhhhhh," he said sagely.
"Ohhhhhhhhhhhhh," echoed Willy.
"AhhhHHHHHHHHHHH," he said loudly.
"AhhhHHHHHHHHHH," echoed Willy.
At last the old man said, "Come closer,
and hold out your hand."

Willy moved forward with his hand
outstretched, and the old man whispered the
name into his palm. Closing his hand quickly
to protect the name, Willy called out his thanks
and raced home to
tell his wife.

He ran down the mountain and over the hills. Suddenly, in the fields on the edge of his village, he tripped on some stubble of corn. He fell ... his hand came open ... and the special name was gone!

Willy looked desperately at the ground. He could see nothing but corn stubble. Now how could he name his son?

He rushed to the village and gathered the strongest men to help him. Back in the field, they all dropped to their knees to search for the name, hoping they would know it when they saw it.

As they were looking, an old woman came along. She peered at the strange scene and called out, "What is happening here?" Willy rushed over. "Oh, old woman," he cried, "this has been the worst day of my life." And he told her everything — how he had grown to be a young man, had fallen in love and married, had visited the Wise Old Man to learn the name of his son, and had fallen and lost the name.

"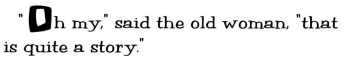h my," said the old woman, "that is quite a story."

"Yes," said Willy. "And now I'll never know my son's name."

"Why," said the old woman, shaking her head, "it's simply ridiculous."

"It is?" exclaimed Willy.

And he rushed home to tell his wife that even though he had lost their son's name on the way home, the old woman had known it.

And so, Willy and his wife named
their son ... Simply Ridiculous.